TAMING THE BIG, BAD Wolf

Olive Spencer

Copyright © 2024 Olive Spencer

All rights reserved. This book or any portion thereof may not be reproduced or used in any manner whatsoever without the express written permission of the publisher except for the use of brief quotations in a book review.

First printing, 2024.
Discreet Cover, 2024.

Ruthless Publishing
807 Holmes Drive, Studio LR
Colorado Springs, CO, 80909

www.olivespencer.com
www.library.olivespencer.com

Also by Olive Spencer

Contemporary Erotica
More than Words
A Dolly for Christmas
A Valentine for Dolly

Paranormal Erotica
Blood Lust
Blood Lust Crimson Temptations
Ghosted

Erotic Romance
Working for the Big Bad Wolf
Taming the Big Bad Wolf
Old Enough to Know Better

Freebies:
Plaything - Working for the Big Bad Wolf
Playing Telephone - Working for the Big Bad Wolf
Blow Me, Harkness - Ghosted
Feeding Frenzy - Blood Lust

Dedication

For the girls who got everything they ever wanted and then got more, this is for you.

Content Warning

This book contains sex between two consenting adults. While Mina may call Grant her 'uncle' there is no blood relation between them.

Contents

Prologue   1
Chapter One   2
Chapter Two   6
Chapter Three   10
Chapter Four   15
Chapter Five   19
Chapter Six   25
Chapter Seven   32
Chapter Eight   39
Chapter Nine   42
Chapter Ten   46
Chapter Eleven   50
Chapter Twelve   54
Epilogue   59

Acknowledgements
About the Author
Where to find Olive Online
Thank You

Prologue

My best friend's daughter is everything I didn't know I needed and everything I never knew I could have. She's been mine since the day she walked into my office, begging for a job. When Mina offered me her body, I couldn't resist. Young, pretty, untouched - it was all I could do not to ravish her in my office.

The moment the partition goes up, Mina has my complete and undivided attention. We steal away for a weekend 'work' trip, but we both know we'll be doing anything *but* working. I plan to give Mina everything she wants and then some.

I don't want to be a simple summer fling.

I want to be the one she comes to for everything.

I want to *be* her everything, and I always get what I want.

I never intended to fall in love with my best friend's daughter, but here I am.

They say when a wolf falls in love, they mate for life…

Chapter One

Mina likes to make a grand entrance. She makes me wait in the town car for five, ten, then fifteen minutes. After twenty minutes, I grow impatient, tapping my fingers on the window. The driver has long since shut off the engine, and he asks me if we should leave. My phone has been silent for hours. The door opens suddenly, and Mina strides out confidently, her roller bag in tow. I sigh with relief when I see she's the only one coming out, and her father hasn't caught on to our little rendezvous. It'd kill hm to know what I have planned for his daughter.

I've known Mina's father, Roger, since college. We were business majors with stars in our eyes and plans to take over the world. I became a billionaire while Roger became a dad. He maintains that that was his plan all along, but I can't help but sense that he harbors a little resentment toward my success. If he knew I was fucking his daughter, I know it would be more than a little. It would end our friendship. It would crush him. And worse? It would devastate Mina.

Mina throws her bag in the trunk and slams the lid.

When she slides into the seat beside me, I can tell something isn't right.

"Felix, would you roll up the partition, please? I need to discuss a private matter with Ms. Maguire."

"You got it, boss. Just tap if you need me." He pushes a button, and the partition rises, leaving us in silence. The sound of the tires on the street fills the tense air between us, and Mina lets out a deep sigh.

"What's wrong, Little Red?" I wrap my arm around Mina's shoulders and pull her to my side. She relaxes into me, and I inhale the sweet scent of her shampoo and perfume. Peaches and gardenias. Enchanting, intoxicating, and arousing, her familiar scent lights a fire inside me. I carefully remind myself of where I am. I can't be caught making a move on Mina in a company car. I have to remain professional, at least in appearance, until we reach the hotel and we're tucked safely into our rooms.

Mina looks up at me with sadness in her eyes. "I got into a fight with Daddy. He refuses to see me as an adult, with a life and career of my own. He still sees me as a little girl, and it's infuriating. Why can't he let me live my own life? Why does he have to control everything?"

"Did he say something?" I ask, already knowing the answer in the pit of my stomach.

"Yes. He didn't want me to go away with you. He said you were taking advantage of me. I think he's starting to suspect us."

Under no circumstances can Roger find out about us. That was the number one rule of our agreement. *Was.* Before I fell in love with Mina, and she turned my entire world upside down, our agreement was simple. Don't tell your dad. Don't let anyone find out. Don't call me *Uncle Grant*. But, of course, all of that went out the window the first time I tasted her. The moment she offered me her body, my life ceased to be my own. Mina became my everything, my only thing. Now, I can't think of a life without her in it. Roger must *never* find out.

"It's going to be okay, princess. You let me slay the dragon. I'll take care of everything, don't worry."

"Thank you, Uncle Grant." Her voice sounds small and far away. She only calls me *uncle* in bed, and I know this argument with her father is weighing heavily on her mind. I would do anything to take this off her shoulders.

"Did you pack something sexy for me?" I try to change the subject and draw her out of the shell she's retreating into. Mina nods and her lower lip trembles. My guts churn. I know what a daddy's girl she's always been and how fighting with her father causes her heartache.

I tilt her head up until her eyes meet mine. Mina blinks a tear away, and her big doe eyes peer into mine.

"I will take care of your father's suspicions. If I have to fire Gladys to keep her quiet, I will."

"No, don't! Don't fire her. She's worked for you for so long, and she needs her job more than I do!" Leave it to Mina to be concerned for others, even when her own happiness is on the line.

"I won't fire her, but I can reassign her to another department. She's far too nosey for my liking, and if she's putting a bug in your father's ear about us, I won't have it. I'll take care of your father, too. I'll set him straight. He won't find out about any of this. I promise." I kiss Mina's forehead, letting my lips linger on her warm skin. A small sigh escapes her lips, and she drops her head to my shoulder.

"Thank you, Uncle Grant."

I know Mina too well by now. On the outside, she's

a grown woman. On the inside, she's a sad, scared little girl. A little girl who needs protection. I wrap my arm around her and hold her closer.

"I'd do anything for you, baby girl. Now, close your eyes. We've got a while before we get to the hotel. You rest, and I'll plan a way to keep your father at arm's reach."

Mina settles in and, within a few moments, she's asleep. Between the emotional car ride and our sexy tête-à-tête in the boardroom this afternoon, she's exhausted. While she rests her eyes, I think of ways to keep Roger at bay while keeping Mina in my arms. I'll throw myself on a grenade if it means I get to keep Little Red to myself.

Chapter Two

"It's time to wake up," I whisper, rousing Mina when we arrive in front of the hotel. She looks up at me through heavy lashes and blinks, slowly coming back from her dreamscape. Mina yawns behind her hand, rubs the sleep from her eyes, and fixes her skirt.

"How long was I out?"

"A few hours."

Mina blushes. "I didn't intend to sleep for so long."

I grin and kiss her cheek. "I'm going to check in. Go to the bar, order me a drink, and I'll be with you soon."

She pulls a mirror from her handbag, straightens her hair, and opens the door. She steps outside gracefully and makes her way inside the hotel. I tip the driver and head after her, collecting our bags and depositing them on a cart to have brought up later. The clerk at the desk checks me in and hands over two sets of keys—one for my room, and one for Mina's. They're individual rooms, but with an adjoining door. We must maintain appearances, but when night falls? Mina is mine. All mine.

I pocket the keys and head for the bar. Mina sits on a

stool, oblivious to the bartender's flirting. I know she only has eyes for me, and my heart swells with pride. Mina sips her martini delicately, the very picture of a sophisticated lady. When I reach her side, she beams at me.

"Your whiskey, Mr. Wolf." She slides the cocktail across the bar, and our fingertips brush. It's the most contact we've ever had in public like this, and it's electrifying. I can't believe how bold she is. I'm surprised she didn't bat her eyes and call me *Uncle Grant* in front of the entire bar. Surely, the jig is up. Everyone knows she's not just my employee.

"Thank you, Ms. Maguire." I smile my most winning smile and slide her key to her discreetly. She tucks it into her handbag and finishes her drink in one dainty swig.

"If there's nothing else, sir, I think I'll call it a night." Mina slides off the stool and heads toward the lobby.

"Goodnight, Ms. Maguire. Back at it in the morning."

"Goodnight, sir." I watch her retreating form as she strolls through the lobby. Her ass looks absolutely succulent in her tight skirt, the long lines of her legs accentuated by seamed stockings and heels. I feel the click of her shoes on the marble floor in my chest—*click, click, click.*

She waits outside the elevator and when she steps inside, she turns to face me. Mina winks as the doors slide closed, and I feel my heart go along with her.

"You're a lucky, lucky man," the bartender says. He leans on the bar, wiping a tumbler clean with a white towel, and I'm sure I've misheard him.

"Excuse me?" I shake my head, staring at him.

"You're a lucky man. A piece like that, calling you 'sir' and 'Mr. Wolf'? What I'd kill to have a babe like that waiting upstairs for me."

I see red. I slam my whiskey on the counter and lean in,

glaring at the young man.

"Listen here, and listen well. She. Is not. A *'piece,'*" I growl. My eyes narrow as my fingers grip the glass. "That young lady is my business associate and, more importantly, my niece. I am in charge of her welfare this weekend, and that includes dissuading lecherous creeps like you from chasing after her. She has a bright future ahead of her, and the last thing she needs is some greasy slimeball ogling her."

I throw my black card on the bar with vitriol. "If I catch you making her even the *least* bit uncomfortable this weekend, I will make sure you no longer have a job."

The bartender stares at my card, then at me, mouth agape. "I will *buy* this hotel and see to it personally that you cease to be employed here. I will make it so that you will never work at any of the hotels in this chain, either. Do I make myself clear?"

The bartender shuts his mouth, nods, and runs my card without a word.

"Good. Now, if you'll excuse me, I'm going to turn in." I tuck my card back into my wallet and push off from the bar. I walk swiftly through the lobby to the elevator and press the button for our floor. I step inside, and my phone buzzes. Pulling it out, I see Mina's face light up the screen.

"I'm on my way, baby girl."

"Good. I don't know how much longer I can stay awake. This bed is so comfortable," she teases. I hear the rustling of fabric, and I know without seeing that she's rolling around in the sheets.

"Hopefully you can stay awake a few more minutes, princess. I've got a bedtime story you don't want to miss," I growl. Her breath hitches and her voice drops.

"What kind of story, Uncle Grant?"

I walk down the hallway and stop in front of my room. I slide the key in the lock and open the door, hanging up the phone.

"The kind where the Big, Bad Wolf fucks Little Red Riding Hood deep into his big, comfy bed. How does that sound, baby girl?"

Mina rushes toward me, and I shut the door. She wraps her arms around my neck and stands on tiptoe, kissing my cheek.

"I thought you'd never come."

"Don't worry, princess. You let me tell you that story, and we'll *both* come."

She leads me to the edge of the bed and pulls me on top of her, giggling as our bodies collide.

"How's it start?"

"Like this."

I bring my lips down on hers, and the world stops spinning.

Chapter Three

Mina is the still point of my turning world. No matter what happens outside of the bedroom, inside these four walls, she is my *everything*. The moment our lips touch, the world feels right. I forget my troubles. I forget my worries. All that matters is the woman in my arms.

We roll around in the fluffy, white bedding, kissing and moaning, our hands exploring each other like it's the first time. We fucked hours ago, but Mina is insatiable. She could go nine rounds and still want—still *need*—more.

"Let's get you out of these clothes," I whisper, my lips on Mina's neck. My fingers toy with the buttons of her blouse. It falls to the sides, slowly exposing her perfect breasts. She mewls as I trail a finger around the shell of her bra and stroke her taut nipple.

"Let's get me out of these clothes." Mina rolls her blouse down her delicate shoulders, revealing a length of silken skin. She looks at me through heavy-lidded eyes while she removes her bra.

"No. Let me." I join her on the bed, swiftly unclasping her bra. I kiss my way down her collarbone, my fingers trailing lightly over her skin. Mina gets goosebumps and whimpers as my fingers twirl around her swollen, pink nipples. Her breasts fit flawlessly in the palms of my hands, and I feel the jackrabbiting of her heartbeat beneath my touch.

Mina pops the buttons of my shirt with practiced ease. She makes short work of taking off my undershirt, tossing it aside while I unzip her skirt and discard her panties. Within moments, Mina is straddling my lap, her pussy grinding against my thigh.

"Tell me what you want, baby girl," I murmur, kissing her neck and stroking her back. I run my fingers over the planes of her skin. My cock taps at the entrance between her legs, the tip swollen and oozing precum. I want to be inside her, I need to be inside her, but I need Mina to tell me she *wants* me more. I need Mina to tell me she *needs* me.

"I want *you.* I need *you.* I want *all* of you inside me."

"What are you saying?" I look her in the eye curiously, trying to catch her meaning. There are so many ways this could go. I want to hear her say it.

"Tell me, baby," I coo, kissing her cheek. I feel her skin burn, and she casts her eyes down.

"I want to feel you dripping down my thighs."

"Baby girl, look at me. If this is what you want, what you *really want,* you don't need to be shy about it. Tell me what you want, always. Tell me what you need, what your heart desires most, and I'll go to the ends of the earth to give it to you."

"I want you to come in me. I want to wake up with it dried on my thighs," she whispers, her voice hoarse with desire. She grinds her pussy on my leg, and we kiss, her tongue exploring my mouth. *Whatever Mina wants, Mina gets.*

"I'm going to fill you with so much cum, it'll be dripping down your thighs for a week." I break away, panting, my cock painfully hard. I lie back while Mina straddles me, her nails gripping me tight as she aligns herself. I position my cockhead and let her slide down my length at her own pace. Her nails dig into my shoulders as she finds her rhythm. I wrap my hands around her waist, steadying her as she rocks. When she finds her pace, I slide my hand down and thumb her clit. Mina whimpers as I lazily stroke her nub, drawing out her pleasure.

"You look so good with my dick inside you, pretty girl."

"Thank you," she whines, eyes shut, head tipped in pleasure.

"What can I give you?"

"Everything. Give me everything, Uncle Grant."

I groan as I withdraw from her slick folds and roll her onto her back. I position a pillow beneath her head and find my footing. Mina guides my cock into her entrance and moans as I slowly push inside. Her legs lock around my ass, holding me close. Mina slides her hand down her body and rubs her clit, drawing tight circles with her delicate fingers.

"I love watching you play with yourself," I grunt, rocking into her faster. My pleasure builds as her core contracts around my dick. I can read her body like a book, and I know she's close. "Let me see you come undone, princess."

Her muscles contract around me, and she lets out a soft moan, mewling my name.

"Let it all out, baby girl."

I find the spot she likes and bury my dick in it. Her cries of pleasure spur me on while I fist my hands into the sheets. Mina locks her legs around me, and I know she's about to come. I stroke her clit, and her body vibrates with need. One more touch, and she'll explode into a thousand pieces of starlight and pleasure. I run my thumb across her swollen nub, and the magic happens.

Mina moans into my shoulder as a climax rocks her body. My climax follows soon after. I thrust inside her, gripping her thighs tight beneath my palms. With one last groan, I push into her and find my pleasure, letting it wash over me. Galaxies explode behind my eyes, and ecstasy rushes through me like an imploding supernova. I've never come so hard in my life. Thick ropes of my devotion shoot inside her.

Draining myself into her hot, tight pussy, I collapse with a long groan, pinning Mina to the mattress beneath me. My head swims, my heart races, and my ears ring thunderously. The world spins like a top around me as I try to catch my breath. *Fuck.*

Mina kisses my shoulder, tracing circles around my spine as I float back to reality. When the room stops spinning and the ringing clears, I find her on cloud nine. With her eyes closed, Mina bites her lower lip in a gesture of pure bliss. Her cheeks are pink as I stroke her heated skin, eliciting moans and whimpers of delight. I trace her stomach and breasts with the tips of my fingers, skittering them along her ribs and collarbones. I reach her chin and caress her cheek. Mina nuzzles into my touch and sucks the pad of my thumb between her bubblegum-pink lips.

I chuckle, kissing her shoulder. "Did you like that, princess?"

Her eyes still closed, she whispers, "Oh, yes."

"Do you like being full of my cum?"

Another, "Oh, yes."

"Are you tired, baby girl?"

"Oh, yes."

I roll my eyes and yawn. "Should we get some sleep?"

"I'm not tired, Uncle Grant," she protests weakly as I kiss her collarbone and roll onto my back.

"Sure you're not, baby girl."

I watch Mina for a while, taking in her blissed-out state. Looking at her, I've never felt my heart so full. Her skin glows from within as she lies beside me. Messy red curls frame her face, and her chest rises and falls with each peaceful breath. I pull the sheets around her, and she tucks herself against my frame, our bodies intertwining. Her legs wrap around mine while my chest presses into her back. I feel her heartbeat. I hear her steady breathing. Her presence soothes me, and soon I find myself falling asleep.

Fucking my best friend's daughter was one thing.

Falling in love with her is another.

Chapter Four

I spend the entire night next to Mina, her soft body curled into mine. I *could live like this,* I surmise in the early morning hours. I tell myself, *I could die like this, and I would go to my grave a happy man.*

When the light streams through the curtains in soft beams, illuminating her sleeping form, I sit and watch her, taking in every inch of my pretty girl. Dappled sunlight streams over the bed, casting her in a captivating *chiaroscuro.* She looks like a Renaissance painting brushed in oil, a goddess in repose, and it takes all my strength not to wake her. I let her sleep and watch while she dreams. Mina. Little Red. My plaything, my *everything.*

I kiss her shoulder as I slide out of bed, careful not to jostle her. When my feet touch the floor, she stirs and rolls over, sleepy-eyed and bed-headed. The sheet falls away and exposes her, nipples soft and peony-pink in the morning light. I want to crawl back into bed and spend hours lavishing her with attention, but I came to work. My responsibilities call, and I have to answer.

"Where are you going?" Her voice is a sleepy siren

song, urging me to come back to bed, begging for five more minutes.

"One of us has to work this weekend, sweetheart. I've got a meeting at ten, and I can't roll into the offices of J. Smith Security smelling like sex."

She blinks and yawns behind her hand. "Oh."

"Stay in bed a little longer, princess. I'm going to shower and get dressed, and then we can go down for breakfast."

Mina doesn't protest. She shifts and rolls into my spot, pulling the sheets around her shoulders. Within moments, she's asleep again. I slip into the shower and let the hot water cascade over my skin. I use the time to think about the deal I need to secure. My plan to keep Mina's father at bay. My feelings for Mina.

Keeping Mina to myself is paramount. I can't let her father know what we've done. I can't ever let him know what *I've* done to his little girl. While my friendship with Roger is important, I can't live without Mina. I wake up thinking of her, and I go to bed the same way. She's my entire world.

I know when she goes back to school in a few weeks, I'll be wrecked. She makes no promises to visit. There are no assurances to come back. She'll go back to Connecticut in the fall, and I'll stay in the city, chained to a desk. Deals will be made, contracts will be signed. The sun will rise in the morning, the moon will come out at night. I will dream of her each night, I will want for her every day.

I could watch Mina sleep all day; she looks so innocent. For a moment, I think about how I've corrupted her. I deflowered her the day I hired her. She sucks my cock while I'm on the phone with the board of directors. I've fucked her on the conference table after everyone has left the office more than once. I *continue* to fuck her even though I know it'll never last. It *can't* last. My heart aches knowing the first time I see her in my bed might be the last.

I dress in silence, moving carefully around the room. When Mina wakes, I'm halfway through sliding into my shoes.

"Slipping out already?"

"I wanted to let you sleep. Are you hungry, baby girl?"

"Starving. Give me a minute to get dressed?"

"Take all the time you need. Meet me downstairs, but use your door. I can't have anyone see you slip out of my room."

Mina nods and stretches again, moaning softly.

"Sleep well?"

"Best sleep I've ever had." She blows me a kiss as I head for the door. "Oh, Uncle Grant?"

"Yes, princess?"

"Thank you."

"For what?"

"For everything. For giving me *everything*."

"Anything for you, pretty girl," I say, smiling warmly. "Get dressed. Don't keep me waiting."

I take the elevator to the ground floor and walk into the atrium. I need to screw my head on straight before this meeting, and the best way to do that is with breakfast. After a few minutes, I spot Mina emerging from the elevators. Her outfit is polished, her hair perfectly styled. She looks every inch the professional. Mina joins me at the breakfast bar and grabs a plate. She slides next to me and flashes me a pearly smile.

"Good morning, Mr. Wolf. I trust you slept well?"

"Very well, thank you. And yourself, Ms. Maguire?"

"I slept wonderfully."

She fills her plate and walks to a table in the back, and I follow. We discuss the schedule of my meeting while she takes notes. She asks questions, proving to be the best assistant I've ever had. Gladys would never be this interested in the inner workings of Wolf Industries. Her curious mind and sharp wit make her irresistible, and I find it hard to focus on work.

After we eat, I have the car called around and lead Mina out under the porte-cochère. Mina slides inside the car gracefully, and I take my place beside her. The driver rolls up the partition and, in the cool privacy, I place my hand on Mina's knee.

"You're doing marvelously, baby girl," I whisper in her ear.

"Thank you, Uncle Grant," she whispers back, kissing my cheek. She swipes her thumb across it, wiping off a trace of lipstick.

"Am I presentable?"

"You look like a million bucks. You're going to kill it."

"Good. Let's go secure this contract."

Chapter Five

I'm forced to kiss J. Smith's ass for the entirety of our meeting to secure the contract with his firm. I detest J. He's a crotchety old bastard and during the entire meeting, I catch his eyes wandering over to Mina. She takes quiet notes and listens to the conversation like a fly on the wall. Mina is the perfect model of a devoted assistant, and I'm proud of how seriously she takes her position.

While I might be the dirty old man who deflowered Mina, J. Smith has a worse reputation. He runs through assistants and female staffers weekly. I've never seen the same secretary at the reception desk twice, and J. always smells like sex. He smells like leather, sweat, and cheap perfume. Even now, he smells like he's come from an office quickie, and I refuse to become that kind of man. I may be fucking my assistant, but I plan to keep her around for a long time.

J.'s eyes wander to Mina once again, and he licks his lips lewdly.

"Say, Grant. If our companies were to merge, would everyone come on board? Your assistant is lovely and would make a terrific addition to my, ahem, retinue. I'm sure I could find a position for her."

I stop him in his tracks, glaring at him, my blood boiling.

"She is not included. Mina is not a pawn to be bought and sold. She is my star employee. And, more importantly, J.? She. Is. My niece." I spit the words in his face, and I hear Mina stop typing behind us. The room goes completely silent.

J. throws up his hands, laughing. "All right, all right, settle down. I didn't mean anything untoward."

"I know exactly what you meant, Smith," I glower, jumping to my feet. "She is not for sale."

Mina rises quickly as I storm out of the small conference room. She follows me as I blow through the office, cursing under my breath. The nerve. The gall. The absolute *balls* on him. I'm positively fuming, and Mina is speed walking to keep up.

I'm sure J. knows better than to follow us. I'm sure he knows he fucked up. I would never have been so bold as to suggest what he was suggesting. I would never cross that line and steal his girls away. I don't want his sloppy seconds; I don't want his soiled doves. To even insinuate that Mina would join him? My blood pressure surges with rage.

"Get in the elevator."

"Yes, sir."

I hold open the door and usher Mina inside. A gentleman holds the door for a lady, but a wolf makes sure it's closed before he plays with his meal. The metal doors slide closed at a glacial pace. When they finally squeeze shut, I round on Mina.

"Turn around, face the doors. Part your legs and lift

your skirt," I growl, and Mina responds quickly. She does exactly as she is told, dropping her bag and lifting her form-fitting skirt over the round cheeks of her ass. She's wearing the sexy, red panties I bought her, and I sigh. "Somebody came prepared."

"I did."

"I want to see how wet your pussy is."

The doors remain closed, and the elevator does not move. I push the button beside her and lock the elevator in place, holding it between floors.

"In the elevator?" Her voice is soft but titillated. Her breath hitches in her throat, but she doesn't lower her skirt. Her legs part more as I close in on her. I lower my lips to the shell of her ear.

"Oh, yes. I want my pretty little toy properly warmed up before we get to the car. I want your pussy dripping down your thighs by the time we reach the ground floor."

"What if someone tries to get on?"

"Then we let them on and keep playing. Can you come quietly, baby girl?"

"I can try."

"Don't try. Do." I slide my palm down the curve of her ass, into her panties, and circle my finger around the entrance to her pussy. I push one finger inside her hot, wet slit, and Mina's legs begin to shake. I stroke her inner walls, curling and swirling my finger inside her. She reaches out to steady herself and with my free hand, I push the button to start it. I push another finger inside her, and Mina mewls like a cat in heat.

"Shh, baby, they'll hear you." Mina has a power fetish, and who am I to deny her? I know how she reacts to watching me work, how it drenches her panties when I take control in the boardroom. I told her I was the wolf in this story, and I fucking meant it.

"Does that feel good, princess? If you stay quiet for me, I'll give you as many fingers as you want."

She whimpers again, pressing her forehead against the door. I push closer, pressing my dick against her ass. My fingers pump inside her, and I praise her for her hard work.

"Good girl, Little Red. You're such a good girl. Is this all for me, baby?"

"Yes. I love watching you work," she whispers, trying to hold back a moan. Her core contracts around my digits like a vice.

"Tell me more." I push my fingers inside her faster as we pass another floor.

"The way you command a room. It gets me... Unh, please?" She slaps her palm against the door. "Please, Uncle Grant?"

"Go on," I growl. "Tell me what it does."

"It makes me burn inside."

"Is that right, baby girl?" I pull my fingers out and slide them up to her clit, rubbing it furiously. She moans, and I kiss the shell of her ear. "Are you burning right now??"

"Yes!" Mina stumbles forward, and I wrap my free arm around her waist, steadying her. I continue to finger fuck my baby as we pass one more floor, the screen counting down levels until we reach the ground. The elevator gradually slows to a stop, and I quickly withdraw my fingers. Mina whines with need, begging me to let her finish.

"Soon, princess," I whisper in her ear, reminding her of our place. I kiss her temple, then straighten up, adjusting the massive bulge in the front of my slacks. She collects herself, pulling down her skirt. The scent of her pussy hangs in the air, filling me with satisfaction.

The doors open, and J. Smith stands outside, a shit eating grin on his face.

"Grant, I've come to the decision that I was wrong about you. You are a man of impeccable moral fabric and— What's wrong with your assistant?"

"Motion sickness. Mina doesn't do well on the descent," I offer. I step out and Mina remains inside the elevator, pretending to be ill.

"Go on, sir, I'll be out in a moment."

"Very well. As you were saying, J.?"

J. looks at Mina and then at me. He grins and continues where he left off.

"You drive one hell of a bargain, Wolf. We'll continue our contract for the next five years... On one condition."

I stare him down, and J. laughs it off.

"The one condition being you tell me where you got an assistant that looks like that."

My jaw clenches, and I remind myself to relax. Offering J. my most winning smile, I extend my right hand and grab his in an overly friendly handshake. The hand that was just inside Mina, the hand that smells like her sex, glides along his palm like a slug. *Fuck you, J.*

"Connecticut. So, we have a deal?"

J. shakes my hand firmly. "We have a deal! I'll have legal draw up the paperwork on Monday. Now, while you're in town, let me set you up for dinner. I'll have reservations made for tonight. I assume she'll be joining you?"

I turn to see Mina step out of the elevator and stroll toward us on shaky legs.

"Yes."

"Very well. We'll be in touch, Wolf. Enjoy your dinner

and your assistant." J. Smith shoots me a knowing smile and it takes all I have not to punch him in the face. He laughs and shakes my hand again before heading back to the elevators.

Mina catches up to me, and I reach to steady her. Her heel breaks, and she tumbles into my arms. I hold her for a moment, staring into her eyes, before righting her and remembering our place.

"Are you all right, Ms. Maguire?"

"I'm fine; as you said, motion sickness. Would you mind assisting me to the car, sir?"

"Gladly. Lean on me."

Mina wraps an arm around my shoulder, and I ease her through the lobby toward the car. She grips me tight as I guide her across the tile floor. I pull her close to my side, and she whispers in my ear.

"I was daydreaming about sucking you off during your meeting."

It's my turn to stumble. Mina never talks like that in public, and it catches me off guard.

"Excuse me?" I choke out, recovering quickly.

"I wanted to show him who I belong to, where my loyalties lie."

"And who do you belong to, baby girl?"

"Only you, Uncle Grant." I tuck her into the car, and she flashes me her soaked red panties. We're playing a dangerous game, but the reward is worth the risk.

"Damn right, baby."

Chapter Six

After the meeting, Mina retires to her room. She needs time to freshen up before dinner, and I need a few hours to myself. While she rests, I search the internet for sex shops. I want to give my girl a night she'll always remember, and I know *exactly* how to do it. A quick search reveals a shop a few blocks away, and I order an Uber to take me there. I can't have my driver see where I'm going and rat me out to the board. This is a *personal* mission.

The Uber drops me off outside the unassuming shop, and I wander inside. It's a menagerie of pleasure and if I had all day, I'd spend it exploring the wares. I'm fascinated by the latex suits and jelly dildos, and the smell of various scented lubes hangs heavy in the air. The cashier greets me pleasantly and directs me toward the aisle with the vibrating toys. I make my way down the wide corridor and peruse the offerings. I look over the boxes of vibrators, magic wands, and suctioning nipple pads until I find precisely what I'm searching for. I grab the discrete box and bring it to the cashier. She tries to sell me on toy cleaner and sanitizing wipes. To appease the pink-haired, nose-studded pixie in front of me, I agree on cleaner.

The car drops me off, and I sneak inside the hotel without anyone noticing. I take the elevator up to the room and imagine Mina's reaction to her gift. I open the door between our rooms and spy Mina asleep in her bed. I insisted she sleep there. I wanted her room to appear slept in, and she's made a fine mess of it. She's buried beneath the white, down comforter, just the top of her head peeking out beneath the bedding. Mina's soft breathing comforts me. For this moment, there are no best friends to suspect us, no business rivals to settle scores with.

I close the door and retreat into my room. We have a few hours before dinner, and I take the time to unwind. I watch mindless TV, flipping through channels before settling on a cooking show. I watch the chef on the show chop, slice, and dice her way to victory before my eyelids grow heavy and I drift off.

I wake sometime later, and the same show is on. I frantically check my phone and find myself relieved when I see the time. We're not late for our reservation. I can't stand being late, and Mina knows it. I hear the shower running in Mina's room and soft, muffled singing. I creep toward the door and poke my head inside. The smell of her familiar shampoo smacks me square in the face. I listen in the doorway for a few moments, catching a few drifting bars of her song. Her voice is lovely, and I wonder why she never sings in front of me. The song ends, and I hear her shut off the shower. The electric buzz of a blow dryer fills the air, and I step back into my room.

I dress quickly, hurrying into my button down and slacks. I wait nervously, listening to the sounds in the other room. When they quiet, I grab the bag with Mina's present and knock on the door, waiting for her. I hear soft footsteps approaching, and it swings open, revealing Mina in the most gorgeous verdant-green cocktail dress I've ever seen. She knocks the wind out of me in one look, and I forget what I'm doing for a moment. I blink rapidly, taking her in over and over.

"Do you like it, Uncle Grant?"

"Like it? You look stunning, Little Red. That green is... *Wow.*" She leaves me speechless. I admire the plunging neckline, exposing the tops of her plump breasts. The dress hugs her curves like a second skin. She's exquisite, and it takes all my strength not to push her against the wall and ravish her right there.

Mina rises on tiptoe and kisses my cheek. Her breasts brush against my chest, and my cock hardens at the contact. She inches down my body and wraps an arm around me, running her fingers through the hair at the nape of my neck. I kiss the top of her head, inhaling her sweet, familiar scent. Wrapped in the moment, I almost forget I'm holding something behind my back.

"I have a present for you, baby girl."

"A present?" She eyes me curiously, one eyebrow raised.

"Go sit, I'll bring it to you."

Mina leads me to the bed, sitting as instructed. She looks up at me with her big doe eyes and I tuck my fingers under her chin, brushing my thumb over her full lips. I pull the bag from behind my back. She looks at it with surprise. Her eyes narrow, and her lips quirk up at the corners.

"What is it?"

"You have to open it."

Mina peels back the paper and peers inside. She looks up at me, then back into the bag, and then at me again.

"Panties?"

"Not just panties. These ones are special."

"How so?" She looks up at me questioningly. "They look like regular panties."

"These are special because *I control them.*"

"You control them?"

I pull a black remote from my pocket and pass it between my palms. Mina watches, rapt, as it bounces from hand to hand.

"Tonight, your orgasms belong to me. I want you to wear these to dinner. If you tell me no, we'll put these away until you're ready to wear them on your own terms. But if you say yes? Your pleasure is mine tonight."

Mina looks me up and down, her cheeks glowing pink. "Really?"

"I want *you* to choose. Wear them to dinner, or don't."

Mina digs in the bag and pulls them out, fingering the lace panties. She fiddles with the vibrating bullet, and I switch it on in her hand. She lets out a half-giggle, half-scream, and I grin devilishly. I lower the vibration speed and let her warm up to it, watching her curiously.

"What do you say, Little Red? Ready to put your orgasms in the Wolf's hands?"

"I'll wear them. Do you think they'll look good with my dress?

"No one will know you're wearing them but me," I remind her with a chuckle. "Take your panties off and leave them on the bed. I want to watch you put these on."

She pushes her dress up her hips, revealing a length of creamy flesh that makes me groan low in my throat. Mina wiggles out of her silky panties, letting them pool around her ankles before dropping them on the bed.

"I'm keeping these as a souvenir of our weekend," I

say firmly. She grins and bends over, giving me a show. I watch as she pulls the new panties up her ankles and slides the lace up her legs, under her dress, and over the curve of her ass.

I take her hand in mine, bringing it to my lips. "We need to set a few ground rules."

"Ground rules?"

"First, if you tell me to stop, I'll stop. No questions asked, no is no. I want you to pick a safeword."

Mina stares me dead in the eye. "*Pamplemousse.*"

"Excuse me?"

"The safeword. Pamplemousse."

I chuckle and roll my eyes. "I wasn't expecting you to have a safeword so quickly."

"What were you expecting?"

"Something like 'Red,' but I suppose pamplemousse works."

"Good. Don't expect to hear it," she says matter-of-factly.

"Never say never, Little Red. Come here."

Mina steps forward and wraps her arms around my neck. My hands slide around her waist, and we sway back and forth in the doorway, dancing to a silent song. I kiss her forehead and resume setting the rules.

"Two. I'm going to control you through drinks, dinner, and dessert. If it gets to be too much, I want you to *use* your safeword. I want to hear it. If you have to scream it in the middle of dinner, so be it. But I want you to use it."

"I told you, I won't need it," she replies, sticking out her tongue. I roll my eyes and chuckle, shaking my head.

"Would you just listen to me, baby? If you tell me to stop, I'll stop. If you tell me to listen, I'll listen. Your pleasure belongs to me tonight, but your body always belongs to you."

"Oh," she says softly. Mina puts her head on my chest as we sway, and I tighten my grip around her. I don't know where my body ends and hers begins until she tilts her face to mine, looking into my eyes.

"Turn it on. I want to feel it."

"Are you sure?"

"Yes."

I press the button, and a smooth buzzing sound fills the space between us. Mina shudders and whimpers in my arms but doesn't say *stop*. I let her adjust to the sensation before turning it up. The speed renders her speechless, and she tightens her grip around my neck. She quivers in my arms, moaning against my chest, and I know it's too much. I back down the speed, and Mina whines, gripping my chest.

"I didn't say the magic word," she pouts.

"We need to save something for later, baby."

"But, but..." She trails off, pleading with her eyes. Desire burns in them, and I know she wants more.

"I know, but we have a dinner reservation to make. Tell me the safeword."

"Pamplemousse."

"Good girl. I'll give you what you want. Just tell me what you *need.*"

I kiss the top of her forehead and tuck the remote into the same pants pocket as her panties.

"We've got a reservation to keep, princess. Slide on your glass slippers and let's go."

My hands slide out from her waist, and she releases me, stepping backward into her room.

"Uncle Grant?"

"Yes, baby girl?"

OLIVE SPENCER

"I'm never going to say it. You can't make me say it."
"We'll see, princess. We'll see."

Chapter Seven

The waiter seats us at a table where we can watch every meal come and go out of the large, brightly lit kitchen. We order our drinks, and the fun begins. We're far enough away from the surrounding tables that even if they could hear us, they wouldn't know what we're doing. I pull the remote from my pocket and set it on the table in front of her.

"Are you ready?"

"Yes." I turn the panties on to their lowest speed, the sound drowned by the dull roar of the restaurant. Mina squirms in her seat, grasping the edge of the table. Her eyes screw shut, and she chews her lip and whimpers while I gently remind her of the rules.

"If it's too much, princess…"

"No!" Mina yelps and then covers her mouth with her hand. She looks around, cheeks burning. "No, don't. I haven't said the magic word. Please, don't?"

"If you insist," I concede. I slide the remote under the table as the waiter brings our drinks. I slyly increase the speed, my finger working the button incrementally. Mina keeps her careful composure until the waiter leaves. Once he's out of view, her eyes snap back to mine, shooting daggers and hearts at the same time. If looks could kill, I'd die the happiest man. I place the remote back on the table.

"Don't you dare."

It's not a challenge. It's a command. She wants more, and there's nothing I won't give her. I press the button, and her eyes flutter. A low whine escapes her throat, and she drops her hand to her lap. I let the panties buzz away for a few moments before cutting them off. They slow to a halt and Mina drags her gaze to meet mine.

"Please?"

"Please, *what?*"

"Please, Unc— Please, Grant?"

"That's who, not what. What do you want?"

"Please, let me come?" Mina pants the words, her need palpable.

"We haven't finished our drinks, princess. What did I tell you before we left?"

"My orgasms belong to you."

"That's right, Little Red. Your orgasms belong to me. You'll come when I decide you're ready."

"Yes, sir." She casts her eyes down, cheeks burning, and a bolt of electricity runs through me. I reach my free hand across the table, weaving it between our glasses and bread plates, and stroke her knuckles in a loving gesture, forgetting where—and who—we are. Our fingers intertwine, and she looks at me with stars in her eyes. If only every day could be like this; if only every day we could play like this.

"You're so beautiful when you want to come, baby girl." I take a sip of my wine and finger the remote. "Tell me, precious. When you go back to school in the fall, will you come back to visit?" I start the vibrator while Mina takes a sip from her drink. She nearly spills the glass of wine down the front of her dress but regains her composure long enough to set it on the table.

She bites her lip, screws her eyes shut, and nods her head. "Yes."

"I'm sorry, princess, what was that? A little louder," I tease, flicking the toy on and off.

"Yes, I will!"

I slowly increase the speed, watching Mina squirm. A high-pitched whine fills the air, and Mina looks around cautiously. Her eyes flash to mine, pleading.

"They can't hear us, baby. Take a sip of your water."

Mina does as she's told, and I smile warmly, patting her hand.

"Good girl."

She chews her lip to keep her cool. Mina takes another sip, and I turn the vibrations down, watching her steady herself with a deep breath. Her eyes open and focus on me.

"Will you miss me when I'm gone?" she challenges, reaching for my hand. I grasp her fingers and lean in, lowering my voice so only she can hear.

"No. No, I will not."

Her face falls, and she looks into her lap. She pulls her hand back, tucking it under the table.

"You misunderstand, little girl. I will not miss you. I will crave you. I will ache for you. I will yearn for you. But will I simply *miss* you? No."

Mina reaches for her wine, taking a careful sip.

"I won't miss you either," she replies, shrugging nonchalantly.

"Go on." I toy with the remote and her eyes flicker to mine.

"I won't miss you at all." I increase the vibrations, and she crosses her leg, her foot dragging along my shin. "My body will ache for you in the middle of the night. I will whimper your name when I touch myself. I will cry for you when I come, my fingers sticky with love. But will I simply miss you, *Uncle Grant?* No, I suppose not."

Mina's body is a coiled spring of need. I know she's ready to be tipped into ecstasy, and I pull her back from the edge, shutting off the vibrator. She sighs as she brings the wine to her lips, narrowing her eyes at me over the lip of the glass.

"Cheers, Uncle Grant."

"Cheer, princess."

Mina sets her glass down in time for the waiter to bring us our plates, and I sit there gobsmacked and ruminating on our conversation. It's easier to play a game when you know the rules. Mina knows what she's doing, and she does it well. She's biding her time, planning her next move. Mina holds my entire world in the palm of her hand, and she knows it. She could make or break me with a word, and she goddamn knows it.

Mina smiles warmly at the waiter as he refreshes her glass. When he leaves, I turn the toy back on, starting at the lowest speed. A cherry-blossom blush rises to her cheeks, and her fingers shake around her fork. She looks at me with fire in her eyes as she takes a bite, her gaze holding mine.

I speed up the vibrator again, and Mina's fork clatters against her plate. Her jaw clenches, and her eyes screw shut, but she still doesn't say the safeword. She whimpers and squirms, but her resolve is strong.

"Look at you, sweetheart. Whimpering with need, desperate for release."

"I'm not desperate," she protests. Her knees clamp together, jostling the table.

"I think you are, baby. I think you want to come so bad you'll do anything."

"You're wrong."

"We'll see." I drop the remote in my pocket while the waiter reviews the dessert menu. I order for the both of us, watching Mina bite her lip from the corner of my eye. I smirk to myself while I order the raspberry soufflé. The waiter retreats and I fix my gaze on Mina, eyeing her with pride.

"You've held it together spectacularly, baby girl." I lean in, tugging on her hand. Pulling her close, I don't care who sees us. "Do you think anyone would notice if I made you come in the middle of this fancy restaurant?"

"You can try."

"Is that a challenge?"

"Yes."

"Oh, Mina, you're in for it now."

I turn the vibrator on, letting her adjust to the speed before pushing it up to full speed. Mina's eyes go glassy while she squirms in her seat, trying to release the pressure on her sensitive clit. I keep my finger on the button, counting down the seconds as her breath becomes shallow and catches in her throat. *Five...four...three...two...*

"Pamplemousse!" she all but yells, and I rush to shut off the toy buzzing at full speed. She collapses in her chair and puts her face in her hands. A few curious diners look our way, and I pay them no mind. Soon enough, they go back to their conversations. I reach my hand out to stroke Mina's arm, and she lowers it slowly, bringing her gaze up to meet mine.

"Baby, baby, there's nothing to be ashamed of."

She shakes her head. "I'm not ashamed."

"What is it?"

"Why couldn't we have played this game in J.'s office?"

Her response has me chuckling, and she slides her hand into mine. I stroke her palm with my thumb, and her eyes never leave mine. "Because he would have insisted on joining in."

"Uncle Grant?" Mina whispers, looking around conspiratorially before leaning in.

"Yes, baby girl?"

"May I come, please?" *Oh, fuck.*

"Using your manners?"

"Yes," she pants, sitting up as I fiddle with the remote.

"I love it when you say please, princess. But that's not up to me. Do *you* want to come in front of a restaurant full of strangers?"

She takes a big breath, eyes locking on mine. "Make me come, Uncle Grant. Please make me come."

I slide the remote into her palm, giving her complete control of her pleasure. "No, princess. Make yourself come. Let me watch you unravel."

I sit back and watch the relief wash over her as she turns on the vibrator. She pleasures herself in a room full of strangers, not caring who sees the ecstasy on her face. The sight of her delight makes me harder than I've ever been, and I palm myself under the table. I can't wait to get her back to our rooms.

When she returns from the heavens, dessert arrives, and the waiter refreshes the wine. Mina devours her souffle before I even take a bite.

"Aren't you hungry?" she asks between sips of wine.

She's tipsy and pink cheeked, and I've never seen her look lovelier. I lean across the table and kiss her, tasting raspberry on her lips.

"Oh, baby, I'm hungry like the wolf. I'm just enjoying the view."

Chapter Eight

Mina lies with her head in my lap on the way back to the hotel. She stares up at me with adoration, fingering my tie. I stroke her hair, and she closes her eyes, sighing contentedly.

"Does tonight really have to end?"

"Baby, you know we have to go back to reality tomorrow."

"I know. Can't we stay like this a little bit longer?"

"As long as you want, baby girl. As long as you want." I smile and run my thumb over her bottom lip. She nips at it and sucks my digit into her mouth, lolling her tongue over the tip. The sensation makes me groan with need. I slide my thumb from between her lips, and Mina's eyes light up like the Fourth of July. She slides her hand down my chest and toys with my belt buckle.

"No, not here," I reprimand her softly, taking her fingers in my palm. I bring them to my lips and kiss each one. "Wait until we get upstairs and then I'm all yours."

Mina stretches, yawning softly. "How close are we to the hotel?"

"Moments away, sweetheart. Can you hold out that long?"

She rolls her eyes and then a soft pearl of laughter escapes her lips. "I'll try, but you're making it very hard."

"Au contraire. I believe *you're* making it hard." I kiss her palm again, pressing it to my chest.

We arrive and Mina sits up, straightening her dress and stepping out. I wait a few moments before following her. We make our way to the elevator, and I catch the eye of the lecherous bartender. He shoots me a lewd grin, and I glare at him. I pat my wallet, and he straightens up, going back to cleaning the glass in his hand.

"What was that about?"

"Protecting an investment. I'm looking to expand my portfolio. How would you feel about being married to a hotel baron?"

She giggles and rolls her eyes, but I'm one hundred percent serious. I would buy this hotel tonight if she wanted. There's not a thing on earth I wouldn't do for Mina. The elevator takes us up, creeping steadily. I wrap my arms around Mina and pull her in front of me, resting my chin atop her head. I catch sight of us in the mirrored walls, and my heart skips a beat.

I've never seen a more perfect picture than this. I decide Mina belongs beside me, in front of me, *under me,* always. My place is with her. I'll do whatever it takes to keep her here. I don't want to know a life without her in my arms each night.

"You smell like sex, baby." I nuzzle into her hair, and she relaxes deeper into my body.

"You smell like Christmas." Her head rests against my arm, and her fingers stroke my elbow through the fabric of my shirt.

"Balsam and cedar. You're right, my cologne does smell like Christmas. Considering I'm the one who comes bearing gifts for good little girls, it's appropriate."

Mina stops stroking my arm and looks at our reflection in the mirror. Her eyes glow, and her cheeks flush carnation pink. "Beautiful, isn't it?" I stroke her cheek.

"We are," she concedes, nuzzling into my arms a moment longer. The elevator reaches our floor, and Mina steps out, grabbing my hand. I follow closely behind her as she makes for her door. I fish the keycard from my pocket and slide it into the lock. The door clicks, and Mina pushes it open, yanking me inside. Once the door shuts, she leads me into the room and pushes me onto the bed. Mina lowers her lips to mine and kisses me softly before righting herself.

"Unzip me."

I trace the gentle slope of her shoulder and slowly unzip her dress, revealing a length of creamy flesh. I've seen her naked dozens of times, but this is *different*. I bend forward and kiss the knobs of her vertebrae, mouthing my way down her flesh as her dress falls. I ease her out of the soaked, lace panties and pull her onto my lap, cradling her in my arms. I look into her face, and the world melts away. I have all I could ever want or need in front of me.

Mina kisses my cheek, murmuring something I can't hear.

"What, baby girl?"

Mina strokes my cheek and trails her hand down my throat to my chest, placing it over my heart.

"I love you, Uncle Grant. I'm in love with you."

The world slows to a halt. Her words fall on me like a ton of bricks.

"I'm in love with you, too, Mina."

Chapter Nine

I undress slowly, letting Mina touch and explore as she sees fit. I take my time kissing her softly, running my fingers across her skin slowly, and whispering words of love in her ear.

You're so beautiful. You are mine. I am yours. I love you. I love you. I. Love. You.

Mina closes her eyes, soaking in my affection. Her lips find mine over and over again as I manipulate her body. She moans and whimpers into my mouth as I stroke her clit and slide my fingers within her. I spread her pussy wide, readying her for what comes later. She flows like water through my fingers as I touch, taste, and stroke my way across every inch of her superheated skin. Mina burns like a supernova in my arms, but I'll be damned if I ever let her go after this. After tonight, she's *mine*.

Her nipples pucker, and her belly trembles. Her pussy, decadently wet, grinds against my fingers as though she can't get enough of my touch. Her pleasure builds with each passing moment. Soon, she's crying my name, her juices coating my fingers. I hold her close as she comes, whispering praise in her ear.

I love watching you come. You're so beautiful with my fingers inside you.

"I want to take my time with you. I want to make this last. I want this to be something we remember for the rest of our lives." I sheathe myself inside her and almost come right away. There's something about being buried in her sweet cunt that sends me into overdrive and sets my body on fire. I feel every nerve in my body light up at once. As pleasure take its course, I focus on her. Mina, my princess. My everything, my only thing.

I rock my hips slowly, punctuating each thrust with a kiss. She accepts them greedily, begging for more. I pick up speed, and she moans into my shoulder, her legs wrapped tight around my trunk. She whimpers as I reposition myself, rolling over her. I line up the head of my cock and sink inside her once more, groaning in delight.

"Don't stop," she pleads, heels digging into my back. "Oh, Grant! Please!"

"Shh, princess. I'm right here," I coo, kissing her forehead as I pound into her. I bring her hand between us and instruct her to touch herself. In a few moments, her eyes roll back in her head. Watching her pleasure herself while my cock is buried in her drives me wild. I lose myself to the sensations of her cunt contracting around me the closer she gets, and I feel the pressure build at the base of my spine. She rubs her pussy while I drive my cock deep inside her, moaning and whimpering with each thrust. My name tumbles from her lips like a prayer as she chases her release.

I thrust into her a few more times before my release crescendos. I moan her name as I shoot ropes of sticky love into her warm pussy. *This must be heaven. There's no other explanation.* I bury my face in her shoulder as I collapse.

Mina's hands wander across my body as I recover. They trail along my spine and over the flats of my ass, down the tops of my thighs and up my ribs. Her fingers skitter, and I shiver at her soft touch. I roll over and pull her into my arms, holding her close. We lie together in silence, soaking in the moment.

"Grant?"

"Yes, baby?"

"What do we do when we go back to the real world?"

"Don't think about that right now. Tell me what your favorite part of the weekend was."

"The weekend isn't over yet."

I chuckle and kiss the top of her head while her hand rests over my heart. "You're right, we still have all of Sunday morning. All morning to lay in bed, order room service, and fuck the sleep out of each other."

"That sounds good. Will you wake me up with waffles?"

"I have an even better idea." I slide my hand down her body and cup her mound, slipping my finger between her folds. "What if I wake you up like this? What if I wake you up with my head between your legs?"

"That *is* an even better idea," she agrees, giggling. Her giggles cease when I swirl my finger around her clit.

"Does that hurt, baby? You've come so many times tonight, I don't want to hurt you if you're too tender."

She looks up at me and bats her eyelashes like a cartoon. "Will you kiss it better?"

"Baby, if I eat you now, what will I have in the morning?"

She rolls her eyes. "Waffles, of course. Haven't you been following along?"

"We will *definitely* have waffles in bed."

Mina quiets, her fingers absently weaving through the gray hair on my chest. Her nails rake down my sternum, sending shivers throughout my body. I'm beyond tired, but I don't want to miss a moment with Mina. Her touch lulls me into a dreamlike state, and I fight sleep with each passing second so I can spend more time with her. One more moment wrapped up in our own little world. It's peaceful here, and I could spend every day like this.

"Grant?" Mina whispers, stirring me softly. I'm near the edge of sleep, her voice luring me back from the calm darkness.

"Yes, precious?" She yawns and pulls the comforter over us, nestling closer into my side. She kisses my chest, places her hand over my heart, and looks into my eyes.

"Tell me you love me."

"I love you."

"I love you, too."

"Can we stay one more night?"

"Baby, we can stay as long as you like. I'll buy this hotel, and we can live here. We can run away together. We can—"

She doesn't make it past my promise of forever before she's in dreamland. I glance down and see an angelic smile playing across the petals of her mouth.

"I'll do anything for you, princess. Say the word, and it's yours."

Chapter Ten

Morning comes early. Mina, so peaceful in my arms, sleeps through the ringing of my first alarm, and I move carefully so as not to wake her. I remember all the times she fell asleep under her father's desk as a girl. I remind myself that that was nearly 20 years ago. An entire lifetime has passed in the blink of an eye, and that little girl is now a grown woman.

Here she is, asleep in my bed, my cum dried on her thighs. The thought is so dirty, I'm almost ashamed. I should be ashamed of the things I've done to my best friend's daughter. I should be shot for the way I defiled her, for the way I continue to defile her. I'm a filthy old man and she's a young, beautiful woman with her whole life ahead of her. A small voice in the back of my brain reminds me she wanted this. She came to me. She. Wanted. Me. Mina is a grown woman, and she can do as she pleases. She can love who she pleases.

I watch the sun rise through a crack in the curtains, the oranges and pinks illuminating the hotel room like a painting. I've been too busy with life to slow down and appreciate the small things, like waking up with a warm body beside me or the way the pink light casts a subtle, rosy hue over the woman sleeping in my arms. I tuck my arm behind my head and stare at the ceiling, counting my blessings. I would never have dreamed that this is how my life would have turned out.

Mina wakes, her fingers sliding up my chest to my cheek and pulling my face to hers. We kiss as though we've woken up next to each other a hundred times. It's soft, tender, and warm. It's the kind of kiss I could get used to. I could wake up like this every day for the rest of my life.

"How long have you been awake?" Her voice is soft and warm with sleep.

"Not long," I lie.

"Did I miss the waffles?"

"No, sweetheart. We can order waffles whenever you'd like," I reassure her, running my finger along the knobs of her spine. She shivers with pleasure and whimpers when I stop.

"Are you sure we have to go back to the real world today?"

"Positive. But we have a little while before then. Why don't you stay here, and I'll go get us some breakfast?"

"I do believe you promised me room service," she says coyly, and I can't help but chuckle.

"You're right, I did make a few promises last night. As you know, I *am* a man of my word. Room service it is."

We order a small feast. Waffles, bacon, sausage, orange juice, coffee. When it comes, we eat as though we've been starved for years. Mina feeds me a bite of her whipped-cream-covered waffle, and I trail a strawberry around her exposed nipple, sucking the sweet, pink juices off her skin. Breakfast in bed turns into breakfast on the floor while I mouth Mina's tits and pussy for what seems like hours.

At noon, we shuffle downstairs separately, Mina taking one elevator while I take another. I walk her to the car and load our bags before going back to check out. The concierge is a kind-hearted old woman, and she smiles as I pay the bill. I cross the lobby and lock eyes with the bartender one last time. He pretends to be busy to avoid my gaze, but once I see him, I stride into the bar.

"You've lucked out. I didn't purchase the hotel this weekend, but if I ever catch you staring at my niece, making untoward comments, or being a general *douchebag,* I will buy this hotel lock, stock, and barrel. Do I make myself clear, young man?"

The bartender nods, setting down the cleaning cloth he's been dusting with. "I'll keep my mouth shut and my eyes to myself, but it's going to cost you. Do you think anyone's going to believe she's your *niece?* We all saw you get out of the car last night, buckle undone and her skirt pushed up around her hips. Uncles don't *do* that to *nieces.* She's either your mistress or a prostitute. Either way, if you want me to keep my mouth shut, it'll cost you."

I bristle at his attempt to extort me but brush it off. I lean forward and put my lips close to his ear. "You're right, she's not my niece. She's my *best friend's* daughter. Mina is the furthest thing from a mistress or a prostitute," I spit, staring him down. "You can try to blackmail me all you like, son, but there's nothing you can do to hurt me. Come Monday, this hotel will be mine. I will own every hotel in the franchise and ensure you never work for them again. Fuck around and find out, pal."

I walk out coolly, striding to the car. I can feel his icy

stare boring into my back, but I pay him no mind. I dig my phone out of my pocket and dial my financier, informing him of the plan to purchase the hotel. He balks at first, protesting loudly in my ear, but acquiesces when I tell him about diversifying my portfolio. When I tell him there will be a boost to his bottom line, he settles down and agrees to have the papers drawn up.

I slide into the car, grinning like the Cheshire Cat. I ask the driver to put up the partition and, as soon as it's in place, I grab Mina and drag her onto my lap.

"What are you so happy about," Mina giggles, wrapping her arms around my neck.

"Oh, you'll see. How would you feel about running a hotel?"

I kiss her, and she melts in my arms. She has no idea what ends I will go to so I can keep her for myself. This is just the beginning. First, the hotel. Then, her father. I'm going to make Mina mine in every way.

"What if I give it all up, baby? Would you like that? We could stay like this forever. We'd never have to go back to the real world."

"Wouldn't that be nice?" Mina stifles a yawn behind her hand, resting her head on my shoulder. "We could stay in this moment for the rest of our lives."

She nestles into my arms for the remainder of the ride home, falling asleep on my shoulder. The entire drive, I touch a small part of her at all times, grounding myself. Somewhere in between the countryside and the cityscape, I make up my mind. I know what I have to do.

Chapter Eleven

We reach Mina's house, and I softly wake her, kissing her forehead.

"Baby girl, we're home."

The driver pulls around the corner to wait, and I assure him it won't be long as I help her inside. She calls out for her dad, and the empty house echoes in response. Mina turns and looks at me mischievously.

"Wanna fool around?" Her voice is full of desire, as though we haven't just spent the last two and a half days fucking every chance we got. I growl and grab her by the waist, crushing her to me. I bury my face in her shoulder, kissing my way up her throat to the shell of her ear.

"Are you saying you want a quickie, princess?" She shivers in my arms. "Do you want something hot and hard before we go back to the real world?"

"I want something to remember you by when we're at work and I can't be more than your assistant. Give me something to think about while I'm filing paperwork. While I'm taking calls. While I'm alone in my bed, aching for your touch."

"Oh, I'll give you something to remember," I rumble, lifting her into my arms. She giggles, and I tighten my grip on her, fingers sinking into her thighs. Mina wraps her arms around my neck while I carry her up the stairs. I push her door open and drop her on the bed, grinning wildly. We undress quickly, throwing our clothes to the floor. Her fingers skitter up my stomach and chest while I sink onto my knees, wrapping my arms around her waist and pulling her close.

I kiss up and down the soft curves of her trembling belly while her hands pan over the plane of my back. Her nails are sharp as they dig into my skin, anchoring me in place. I glide my hands over her body, licking, kissing, and sucking my way from tit to tit, form collarbone to clit. I latch on to her pussy and pleasure her with my tongue until her knees wobble, and she falls onto the bed, pink-cheeked and panting. She spreads her legs wider, and I worship at the apex of her thighs until her juices run down my chin.

Climbing up her body, I bury my face in the crook of her neck. I inhale her scent, letting it burn into my brain. I want to remember every minute of this for the rest of my days. I want to dream about this. I want this instant to flash before my eyes when I die. She is my nirvana, and this is pure bliss.

We kiss deeply, my fingers exploring like pilgrims in the Promised Land. She begs for more, she begs for harder, she begs me not to stop. Mina whimpers and moans as I play her like a Stradivarius, drawing out the most beautiful sounds of pleasure from within her. Her body responds to my touch in kind, clenching and contracting around my fingers like a vice. She cries my name when she comes undone, and I could listen to her song for eternity. I want mine to be the only name she cries out in her moments of pleasure. I want my cock to be the only one she thinks of in the midnight hour. I want to be the only one she ever needs.

When I withdraw my fingers and pull my pants down, she looks up at me with such lust it almost breaks me. Her thighs part, and her juicy, pink pussy comes into focus between us. I spit on her swollen nub and drag my cockhead through the slick of our juices. She whines with need, squirming beneath me. I swirl my fingers around in our juices, spreading her lips. Her pussy is tender from her release, and she cries out when I run my thumb over her clit.

"I'll be gentle, princess," I coo, reassuring her with kisses.

"Don't be gentle. Just fuck me, Uncle Grant."

I stroke my cock before lining it up with her cunt and closing my eyes. I slide my cockhead along her slit, trailing my precum over her lips. I press inside her in one slick motion, pushing our hips together as I feel her warmth surround me. The moment we're joined as one, all that matters is that we do not stop.

We make loud, passionate love in her childhood bed. The springs creak, the headboard wobbles, and the wooden legs shift and scratch the floor. We become a tangle of limbs and sheets while the soft sounds of moans and sighs fill the air. Mina's body is soft and pliable beneath my frame, bending when I bend, moving when I move. When I come inside her, pinning her to the bed, she grips me like a vice. She latches on to me with legs and hands and teeth. Her hips line up with mine as I shoot inside her, our bodies pressed together like jigsaw pieces. She cries out, the sound music to my ears, and

OLIVE SPENCER

I bury my lips in the crook of her neck. I drain myself, shooting every last drop of cum into her cunt until I feel it dripping down the sides of my cock as I withdraw.

Mina wraps her body around mine. Her fingers trace shapes into my back as my heartrate slows. She whispers love words into my ear, praising me for my performance. She tells me how good it was, how much she loves me, how happy I make her. Her soft words bring me back into orbit from all new heights. My heart pounds against my ribs and I feel the soft rise and fall of her belly as she lavishes me with love and devotion. My head lolls against her shoulder as we revel in this microcosm of satisfaction.

I never, ever want this to end. I don't want to go back to the real world. If I could live in this precise moment in time for the rest of my days, I would go to my grave a happy man. Here, I have all I need. Here, I have my Mina, my everything. What more could a man possibly need?

We're so wrapped in post-sex bliss that we don't hear the approaching footsteps. We don't hear the creak of the floorboards in the hallway, or the click of the handle as it turns.

What do we hear? A roar of anger and surprise.

"Get the *fuck* off my daughter!"

Chapter Twelve

Roger rushes through the door, fuming with indignation. He grabs me by the shoulder and jerks me out of the bed, throwing me across the floor. I scramble to my feet and grab him, spinning him around to face me.

"Roger, stop!"

It takes a moment to register who I am but, when it does, a look of abject horror crosses his face.

"You fucking *bastard!* That's my daughter!"

He closes in on me, and I see the unbridled anger burning in his eyes like wildfire. He backs me against the wall and corners me, his mouth contorted with rage. He spits at my feet and pushes me into the wall with his meaty palms, my shoulders connecting with a thud.

"How could you? You've known Mina her entire life!"

"She's an adult, Roger! Let me explain! We're not—!"

The last thing I remember is the lineup and the crack of his fist connecting with my jaw. After that, the room goes pitch black, and my ears ring like hell.

I come to on the floor, waking up to the sounds of Mina sobbing and apologizing over and over. She wails while I clear the stars from my eyes. Roger turns and glares at me with murder in his eyes. I've never seen him this mad. In twenty-some years, I've never seen him so angry. I've never seen him so betrayed. I only have myself to blame.

"How long has this been going on?" Roger fumes, his voice full of vitriol.

Mina looks up at him. "Since May."

"How long has this been going on under my roof?"

"This is the first time, Roger. We've never—" He glares at me, his hand balling up into a fist again. I prepare for him to swing on me, bracing myself for contact.

"I didn't ask you, fucking bastard. I can't believe you would do this to her. To me, to our *family!* You've known Mina her whole life. Have you been waiting for this since she was a child?"

I scramble to my feet, instantly regretting the motion, but I press on.

"How could you do this, *Wilhelmina*? Rutting around this house like a common whore! And with your *uncle!*" He spits and sputters with rage. "You're going to quit your job, right now, and stay the hell away from him!"

Leaning over him with imposing authority, I clench my teeth and whisper in my fiercest tone.

"Listen here, Roger. I would never have touched her as a child. I didn't even recognize her when she came into my office," I growl, pushing him into the wall. "You may refuse to accept this, but Mina is a grown woman, Roger. She can make up her own mind. And for fuck's sake! I. Am not. Her. *Uncle!*"

His eyes narrow, and his face reddens as he stumbles over his words.

"How the *fuck* could you do this? She's my daughter,

Grant. My fucking daughter! You were there when she was born. You've known her for her entire life. How could you do this?"

Mina sobs behind us. I never intended for us to get caught. I never wanted her to feel like this, to feel like it was her fault. I back away from her father and glower at him. He starts toward Mina, and I grab him, pushing him against the wall.

"Stay. There."

He lands with a thump and, for a beat, I feel bad. Not bad enough to apologize, but bad.

Mina wails, and I turn my attention to her. I sit on the bed and pull her to my chest. She buries her face in my neck and wails, her body shaking with each labored sob. I wrap my arms around her, using my body to shield her from whatever comes next.

"You fucking bastard." Roger spits at my feet, wiping his mouth with the back of his hand. He storms out, slamming the door with such force that the house feels like it's shaking.

I dry Mina's tears and, eventually, her shaking ceases. She hiccups a few times, and I keep her tucked in my arms during the heavy silence. As the last of her tears dry on my shoulder, she pushes away and looks at me with such pain, it rips me in two.

"We can't do this anymore," she whispers, wiping her eyes.

"I know, baby girl. We can't sit on this anymore, and we—" She cuts me off, shaking her head. More tears well up in her eyes.

"No, we can't do *this* anymore." She gestures between us, and suddenly I catch her meaning. "We can't sneak around anymore. We can't *be together* anymore. It's time to end it."

"End it?" I don't want to end it. I don't want to lose her, and I don't want to give her back. I want to keep her for the rest of my life.

"But Mina, I—" She puts her hand on my chest, looking up at me with pleading eyes.

"Please, Uncle Grant. I can't do this. I can't be with you like this."

"Mina, please. I love you. I love you so much. Please," I beg. Tears well in my eyes, and she shakes her head.

"I love you, too. But I can't look at you, I can't look at *myself*. I can't do this. We can't do this. You need to leave."

"Baby, please. I don't want to live without you. Mina, I'm begging you."

"You need to go, Grant. *I* need you to go."

Mina looks miserable, and I've never felt this much pain in my life. I never wanted to hurt her. Guilt wracks my body, and I choke on my own heartbreak. Mina stands in front of me, crying as though she's lost her first boyfriend. I can't do anything to fix her first heartache because I'm the one who's caused it.

I dress in a hurry, throwing on my clothes haphazardly. I pull Mina to me, one last time, wrapping my arms around her. Her eyes are full of tears, and I feel like the biggest bastard on earth.

"Grant, please, just go home," she pleads, sniffling.

I look into her eyes, and the words tumble out of my lips before I know what I'm saying.

"Marry me, Mina. Let's run away and get married."

She shakes her head. "Go home, Uncle Grant."

I kiss her goodbye, my lips lingering on her forehead. The walk to the car is the longest of my life. I apologize to the driver and instruct him to take me home. The partition is barely in place before the first tear falls. By the time I'm home, my eyes are red and puffy, and my shirt is soaked with regret.

I tell myself I should have fought for her. I should have stayed. I should have done more. I should have, I should have… None of it matters now. Mina made up her mind and when she wants something, I'm powerless to say no. She wants me out of her life, and I will give her what she wants, no matter how much it pains me.

I don't know what my life looks like without Mina. I don't know what my world looks like without her in it. I don't know what I'll do without her. When she made up her mind, she tied my hands. Whatever Mina wants, Mina gets. Even if that's a life without me in it.

Epilogue

On Monday, Mina does not return to work. She hands in her resignation via email, and HR cleans out her desk. Every hope I have of fixing everything is dashed. Her empty desk haunts me every day, reminding me of what I've lost. By Friday, Gladys has her position reinstated, and she falls into her old, haughty routines.

Weeks pass, and summer turns into fall. The leaves change, and the weather becomes cool. I look at the calendar and know she's tucked safely away in Connecticut, finishing her degree. It takes every fiber of my being not to drive there every night, snatch her into my arms, and make this *right*. She would have gone back to school regardless of our relationship, but part of me knows she went back in *spite* of it.

Roger never speaks to me again. Texts go ignored, and I'm met with a middle finger emoji. In my gut, I know it's for the best. I lie to myself and say it wasn't sustainable, feeding myself platitudes I don't entirely believe. I can't have my cake and eat it, too.

On a dreary Tuesday in October, Gladys comes into my

office, her nose in the air. She slides a memo across my desk, telling me there's a meeting in the boardroom at one. An impromptu meeting of the board, questioning my position within the leadership of the company I built, I'm sure. I throw it away. They can remove me for all I care. The moment Mina walked away, I lost interest in running this company. I lost interest in everything, All I cared about was *her*. The one person on earth who made me feel alive now makes me feel worse than dead.

At noon, my cell phone buzzes, and Mina's name flashes across the screen. My heart jumps into my throat as soon as I see it. I scramble to answer, fumbling and throwing it across the desk. It buzzes again, and I hurry to push the button.

"Little Red?" I hold my breath while I wait for her response, my heart racing. My stomach flips, and I feel like I might throw up. I haven't been this nervous since I was a much younger man. I haven't had anything to lose since then that was as important as Mina. My heart races as the moments tick by.

"Uncle Grant," she breathes. "I was worried you wouldn't take my call. I know you're busy, and I don't want to intrude."

"You're never intruding, Mina, you know that."

"Thank you." Her voice is small and scared. Something is wrong.

"Are you all right, sweetheart? Talk to me."

I can feel the tears running down her cheeks like a fist to my core. She hiccups, and I can feel it wrack my body. She sniffles, and my nose twitches. Something is off, something is very off.

"Mina, what's wrong? Did somebody hurt you?"

"No, nobody hurt me. Uncle Grant, I need you to come

get me. I need you to come get me right now."

"I'm on my way." Fuck the board meeting. The only thing that matters is Mina. She sounds like her whole world has collapsed at her feet, and I need to be the one to pick up the pieces. I *have* to be the one to pick up the pieces.

"Can I stay with you, Uncle Grant? Daddy doesn't want to see me. He won't speak to me or take my calls. I have nowhere else to go and I—"

I cut her off, agreeing in an instant. "Of course, baby, stay as long as you need. My home is your home."

She hiccups, her voice softening to a whisper. "Is forever too long? I can't go home."

"What are you saying, baby girl?" A pit forms in the base of my stomach, and I already know her next words. There's only one outcome here.

"I'm pregnant," she chokes out. My heart aches as it rises into my throat. I swallow my anxiety, grabbing my keys and coat. I want to wrap my arms around her. I want to kiss away her tears and tell her everything will be all right.

"I'm on my way. I'll be there soon."

"Thank you," she sobs, her voice quavering.

"For you, I'd go to the ends of the earth." My voice softens in the mouthpiece, whispering her name. "Baby girl?"

"Yes?"

"Marry me. Let's run away together. Marry me."

"Please, just bring me home," she sobs.

"I'll be there before you know it, baby girl."

"Thank you, Uncle Grant."

She sniffles as she hangs up the phone, and I feel my spine harden. My princess needs a white knight, and I'll be damned if I let her down.

I rush out of the office, ignoring Gladys' protests. She runs after me, clucking about the board. I stop in the hallway and turn, facing her with a glacial stare.

"Consider this my formal resignation." The office goes quiet as I storm past the cubicles. I don't give a fuck anymore. I don't give a fuck about this job or the company I built from the ground up. It can burn to the ground for all I care. I don't give a fuck about anything. All that matters is getting to Mina and bringing her home.

Before I know it, I'm in my car, pointing it toward the sleepy college town. I roar down the highway at breakneck speed. In two hours, I'll be reunited with Mina, my everything. The woman I love, the mother of my child.

OLIVE SPENCER

Acknowledgements

Once again, I want to thank my friends in a very specific Discord server for encouraging me to write.

I am eternally grateful to the makers of Diet Coke, for without their nectar of the gods, I would not have had been able to focus long enough to get Grant and Mina's story on the page.

I owe a large debt to the creators of Youtube, my friends on Twitter, and the few people in real life who know who Olive Spencer is.

For everyone on Radish, this one is for you.

Thank you, each and every one of you.

About the Author

The Wolf series is one of Olive's favorite tales to date. The idea for the story came from an unused script in her former life as an erotic audio scriptwriter. Having retained the rights to the story, Olive felt it was finally time to release The Wolf and see where the story takes her.

Olive Spencer writes contemporary, and sometimes paranormal, erotic fiction. When Olive is not busy behind the screen of her trusty MacBook, you can find her with a Diet Coke in hand while watching a soap opera, or wandering around a local bookstore with her headphones on.

She's probably listening to a spicy audiobook, or her favorite country song, 'Dicked Down in Dallas'.

Olive is not a Gemini vegetarian, but she is a fan of all things Reese Witherspoon.

Where to find Olive Online

Olive Spencer loves Twitter! Please consider joining her at @misskmagpie and sending her a tweet.

She also thrives on the sense of community and encouragment that comes from publishing on Medium.
Join her at www.olivespencer.medium.com and see what all the fuss is about. If you liked Ghosted and Blood Lust, make sure you read her sleep demon stories!

If you want to visit her website, you can find Olive online at www.olivespencer.com.

Thank You

If you're read this far, you deserve a cookie, a glass of warm milk, and a blanket. Thank you so much.

This is the middle of Grant and Mina's story. I hope you stick around for part three.

www.ingramcontent.com/pod-product-compliance
Lightning Source LLC
LaVergne TN
LVHW061048070526
838201LV00074B/5220